P9-DMS-093

To Richard Thompson—
a big guy in my book

ISBN 978-0-545-84345-4

12 17 18 19 20/0

Printed in the U.S.A. 40

First Scholastic printing, February 2015

An ELEPHANT & PIGGIE Book

SCHOLASTIC INC.

by Mo Willems

A Big Guy Took My Ball!

Gerald!

I found a big ball,

and it was *so* fun!

And then a big guy came—

and—
and—
and—

HE
MY

TOOK BALL!

I am so upset.

That is not good.

That is not right!

Big guys have *all* the fun!

What about
the little guys!?

What makes those big guys think they are so big?!

Their size?

WELL, I AM
BIG TOO!

I will get your
big ball from
that big guy!

My
hero!

Here I go!

Let's see how big
this "big guy" is!

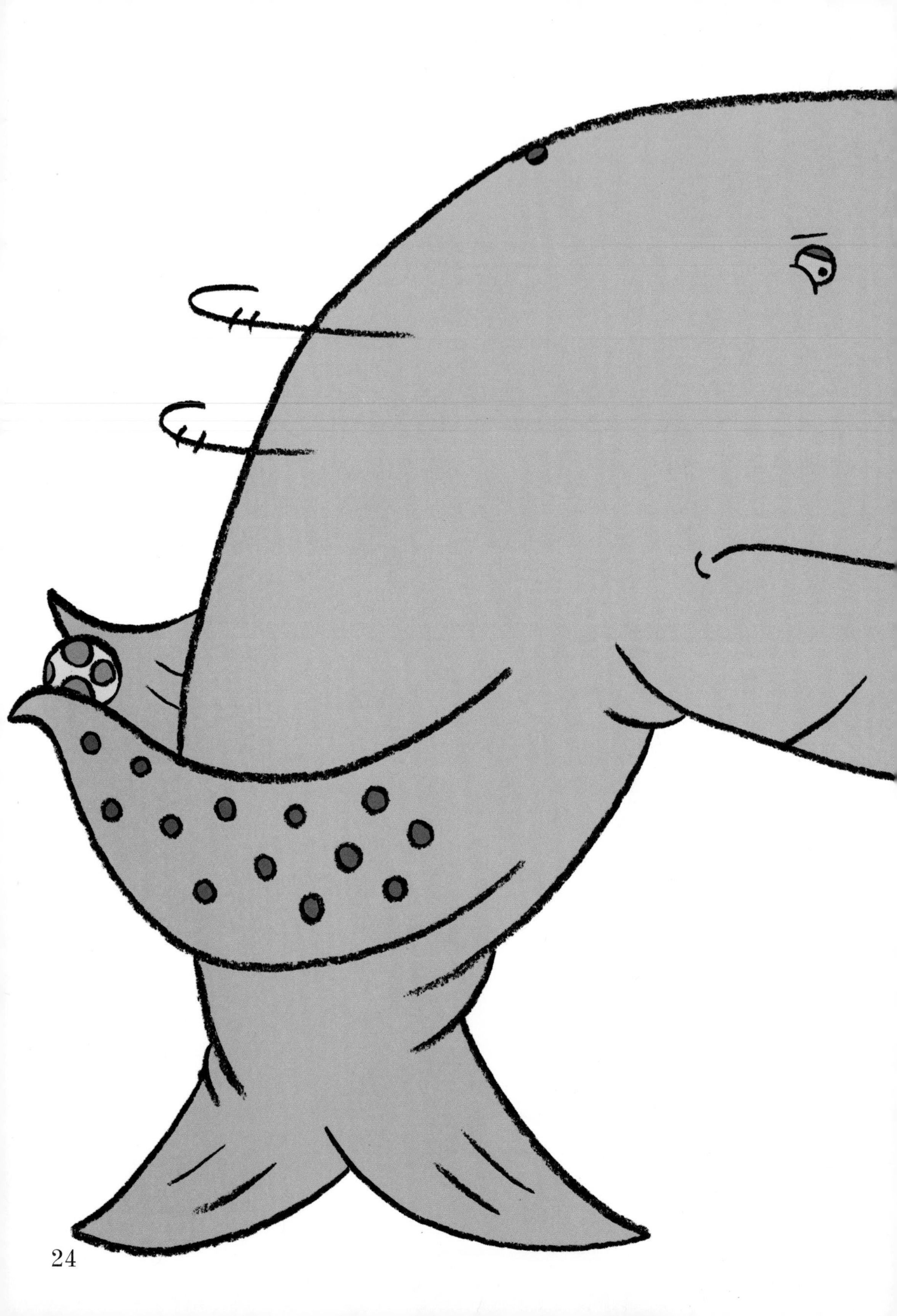

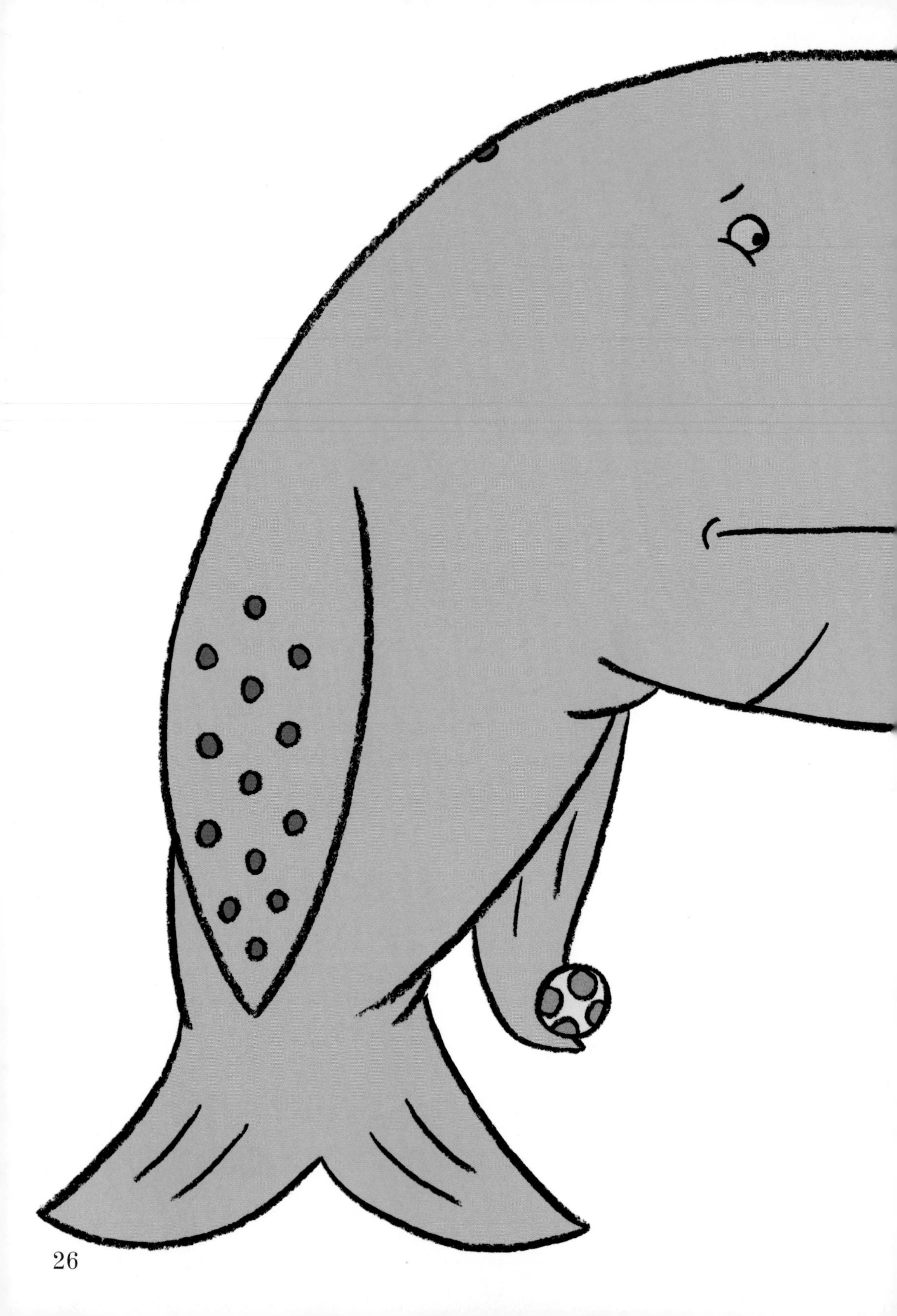

Did you get
my ball back?

That is a
BIG guy.

You did not say
how big he was.

He is very
BIG.

He is bigger than I am.

Much bigger!

I am smaller than he is.

Much
smaller.

He is so BIGGY-
BIG- BIG-

Gerald.

You did not
get my big ball
back, did you.

I did not.

EXCUSE

ME!

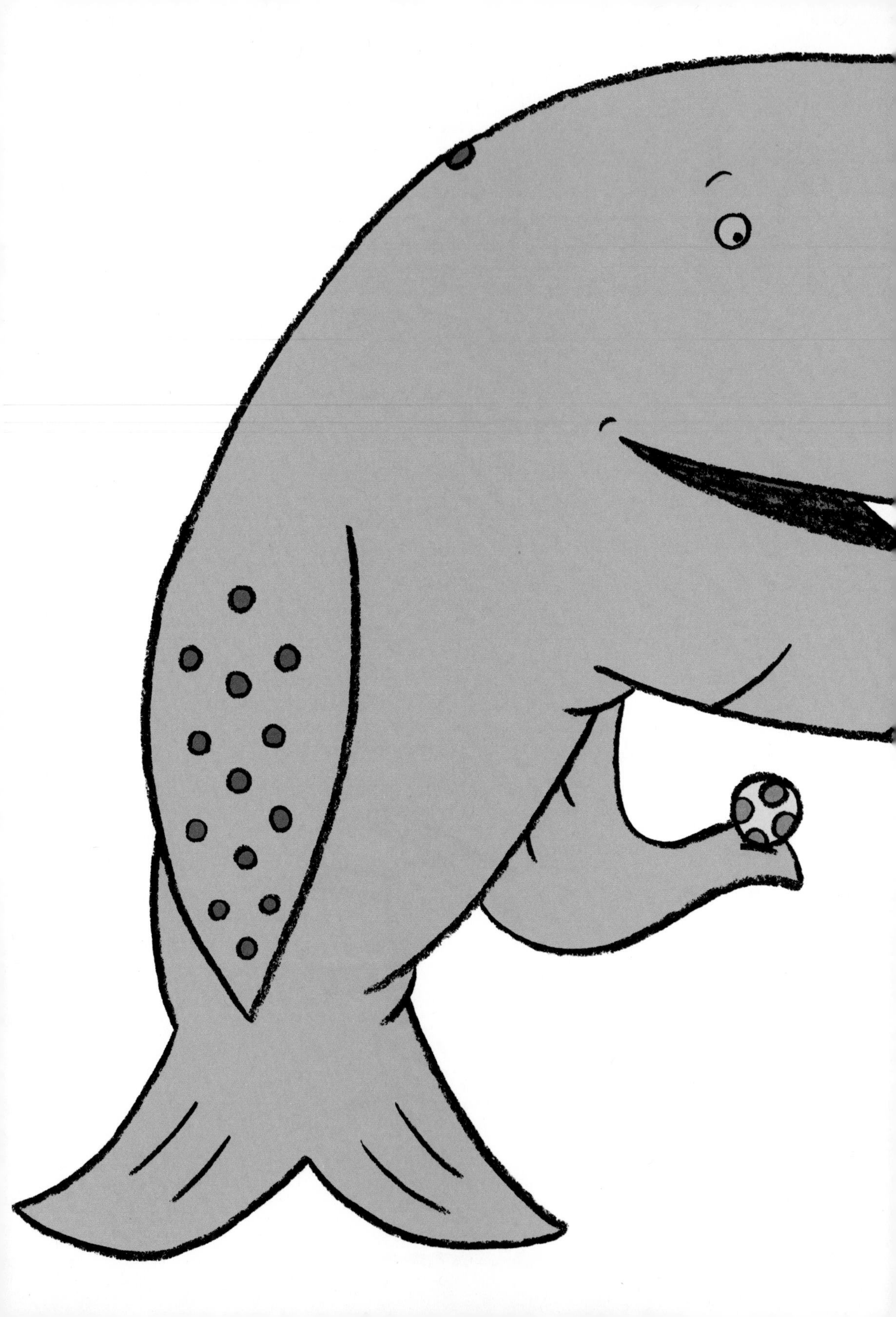

THANK YOU FOR FINDING MY LITTLE BALL.

That is *your* ball?

And you think it is little?

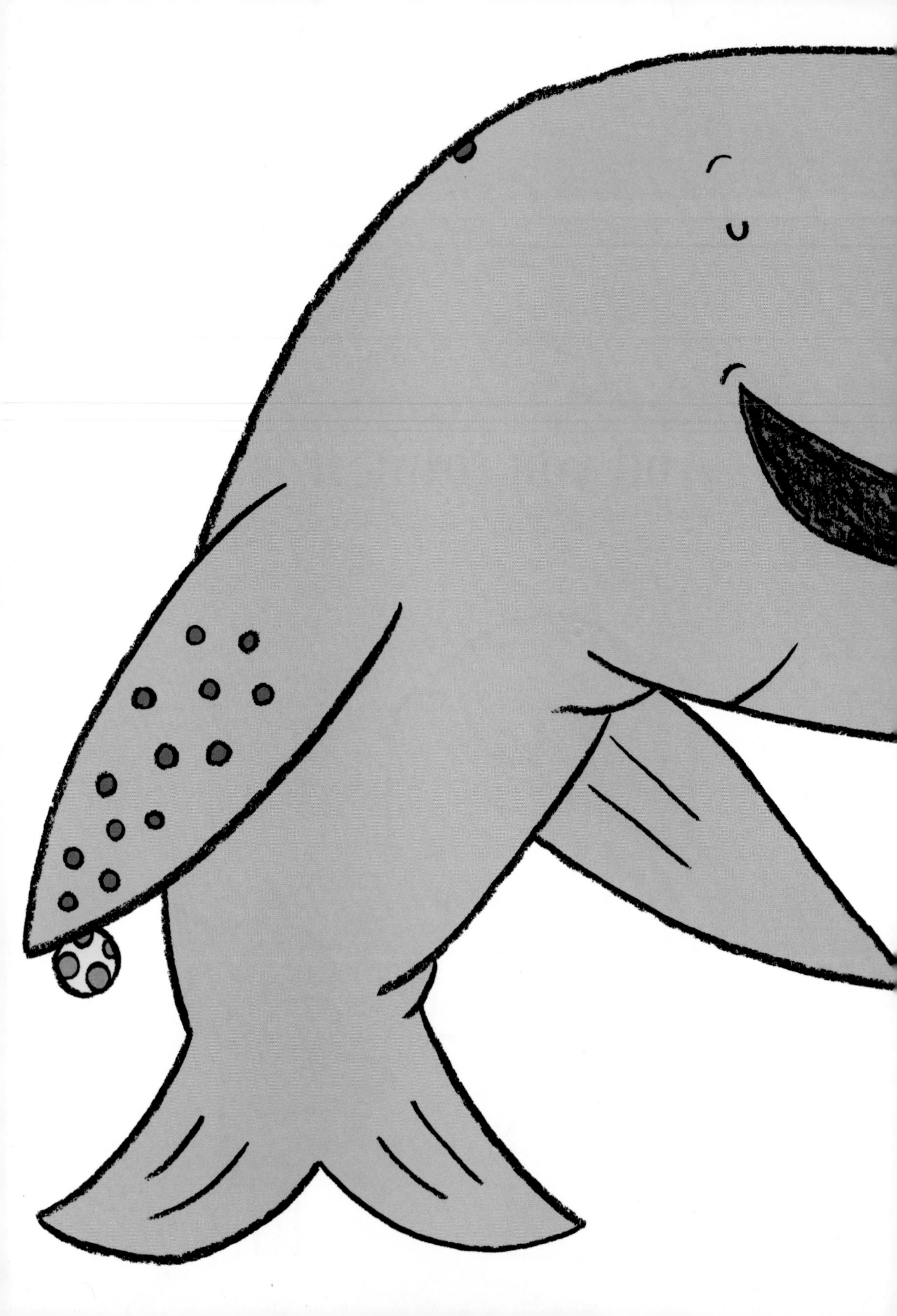

WELL,
I AM
BIG.

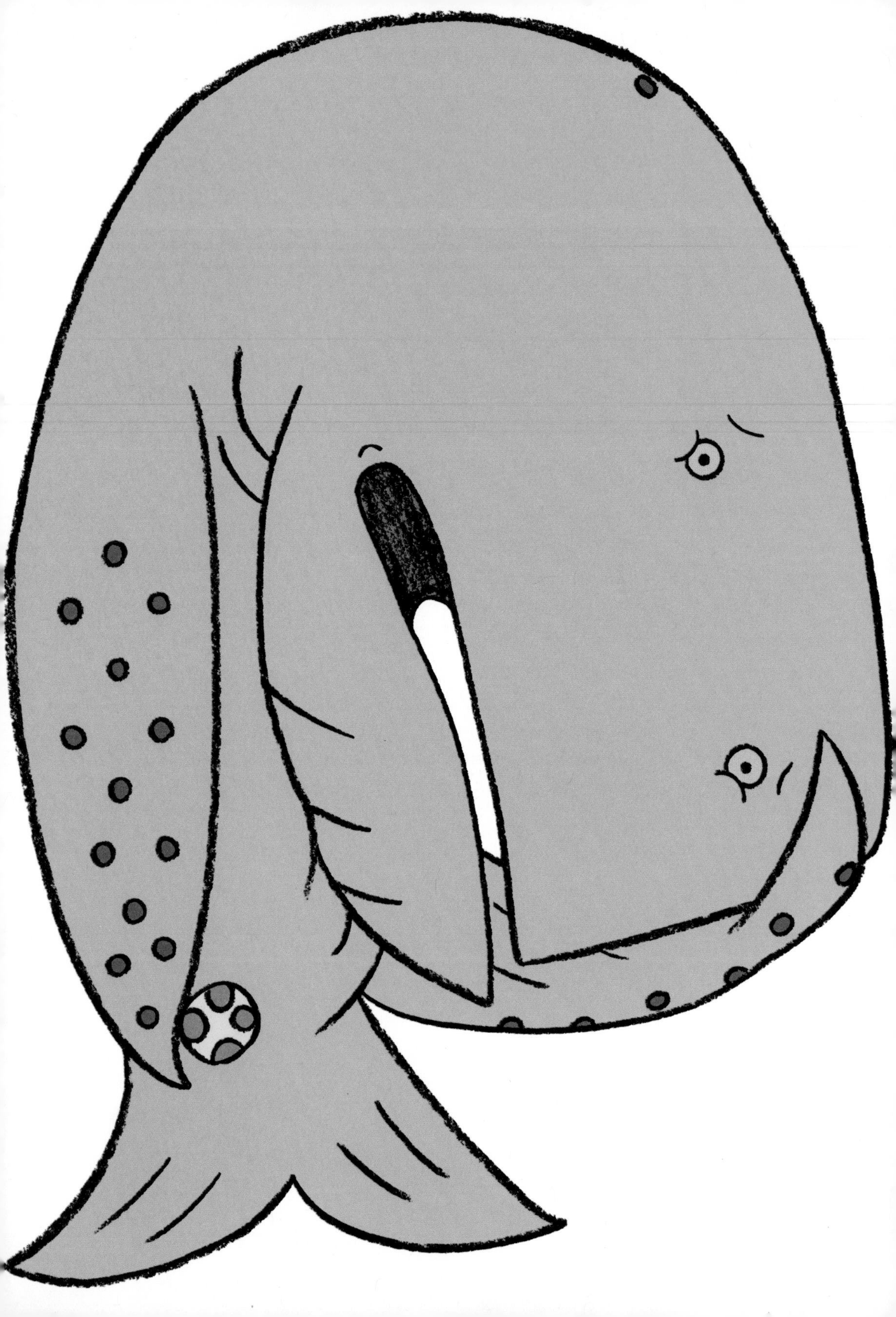

SO BIG THAT NO ONE WILL PLAY WITH ME.

LITTLE GUYS HAVE
ALL THE FUN.

Um . . .
Big Guy!
Would you
like to play
"Whale Ball"
with us?

WHAT IS
"WHALE
BALL"?

We do not
know!

We have
not made
it up yet!

With a *little* help,
we can all have

BIG FUN!

Elephant and Piggie have more funny adventures in:

Today I Will Fly!

My Friend Is Sad

I Am Invited to a Party!

There Is a Bird on Your Head!
(Theodor Seuss Geisel Medal)

I Love My New Toy!

I Will Surprise My Friend!

Are You Ready to Play Outside?
(Theodor Seuss Geisel Medal)

Watch Me Throw the Ball!

Elephants Cannot Dance!

Pigs Make Me Sneeze!

I Am Going!

Can I Play Too?

We Are in a Book!
(Theodor Seuss Geisel Honor)

I Broke My Trunk!
(Theodor Seuss Geisel Honor)

Should I Share My Ice Cream?

Happy Pig Day!

Listen to My Trumpet!

Let's Go for a Drive!